HALLOWEEN

Written and with photographs selected by
KATHERINE LEINER

Mark Hanauer

Atheneum **1993** *New York*
Maxwell Macmillan Canada
Toronto

Maxwell Macmillan International
New York Oxford Singapore Sydney

Special credits:
Photograph by E. J. Camp
    Stylist: Phillip Shubin
    Makeup: Maria Verel
    Studio: Industria Superstudio
    Location: Restaurant Florent

Photograph by Phyllis Galembo
Courtesy of Polaroid

Photograph by Sally Mann
    Copyright Sally Mann, courtesy of Houk Friedman Gallery, New York, New York

Photograph by Mary Ellen Mark
    Courtesy of Mary Ellen Mark Library

Photograph by Lisa Powers
    Child: Chloe Lor
    Makeup: David Michaud
    Hair: Victor Hutchings
    Location: Golden Dragon Restaurant, San Francisco
Special thanks to: Tat Wong Kung Fu Academy, Sandy Sakate of Obiko, and Pam Lor

Photo by Barbara Van Cleve
    Child: Martin Christopher Espinoz, Chimayo, New Mexico

Atheneum
Macmillan Publishing Company
866 Third Avenue
New York, NY 10022

Maxwell Macmillan Canada, Inc.
1200 Eglinton Avenue East
Suite 200
Don Mills, Ontario M3C 3N1

Macmillan Publishing Company is part of the Maxwell Communication Group of Companies.

First edition

Printed in USA

10 9 8 7 6 5 4 3 2 1

The text of this book is set in Cochin.

Book design by Patrice Fodero

Book production by Daniel Adlerman

Library of Congress Cataloging-in-Publication Data

Leiner, Katherine.
    Halloween / by Katherine Leiner.
      p.   cm.
    Summary: Photographs and text capture children sporting a variety of Halloween costumes, including a witch, vampire, princess, and pumpkin ghost.
    ISBN 0-689-31769-7
    1. Halloween—Juvenile literature. [1. Halloween.] I. Title.
GT4965.L37   1993
394.2′683—dc20
                       92-39343

*This book is dedicated
to all children with AIDS*

—KL

Graham Nash

Acknowledgments

I am grateful to all the photographers who so generously donated their time, effort, and their wonderful art. And also to those children who were photographed—most of them knowing that this book would help raise money for children with AIDS. All of you are examples of the kind of love that people can give when they are called upon to help.

My special thanks to: my husband, Miles Budd Goodman; Lynn Eames; Sue Gooding; G. Ray Hawkins; Gail Hochman; Marianne Merola; Tim Sexton; and my editor, Jonathan Lanman, who was looking for a way to help—and has. And, of course, to my children, Makenna Goodman and Dylan Leiner.

Jean Schubach Gewirtz

Introduction

One Halloween night, a long time ago, I was a gypsy.

I wore a brightly colored skirt to my ankles, a silky blouse, and lots of sparkling, noisy jewelry.

I rode a wild gypsy horse, and I lived in a gypsy caravan. That night, everyone sang and danced, and the yellow glow of candlelight shown through our wagon's wooden slats. When the morning dawned, our strong gypsy horses pulled our wagons to the next village.

I was so mysterious because I knew a lot of gypsy secrets.

Halloween is a time when all of us can be someone other than who we are. The children portrayed in the photographs that follow have that in common. Each has been captured on film by one of the leading photographers working today—some caught candidly, some posed, some in elaborate costumes, some in the most simple ones. But what comes through is the diversity and magic of Halloween. Some of the photographs were taken especially for this book, while others came from the photographer's files. Although I did not interview these children, I can remember that magical night when I was a gypsy, and I can imagine, too, what these children might have told me if I had interviewed them.

—Katherine Leiner

The Pediatric AIDS Foundation helps many children and their families.

The Pediatric AIDS Foundation gives money to researchers so they can study and find answers on HIV/AIDS in children. To do this they need lots of help. People hold fund-raisers for them and many other events to raise money. All different kinds of people can help. Many celebrities try to help, many senators try to help, many regular people, and lots of kids, too.

The Pediatric AIDS Foundation can answer almost any question you have about HIV/AIDS. They know and care a lot. They teach many children and grown-ups how you can and how you can't get this virus.

The Pediatric AIDS Foundation brings hope to many children with HIV/AIDS around the world.

Francesca DeLaurentis
Age: 10

E. J. Camp

Here's what cowboys do:
   Ride bucking broncos
   Shoot bad guys—*bang!*
When you're a cowboy, everybody stays
out of your way.
   Everybody!

C H U C K   G A R D N E R

Photographer

In New York City, it's so much fun to trick-or-treat.

We go in a big crowd and we hold hands.

We stop at Kowalski's Bakery, Sandy's Sweet Tooth, and the Creamery. Everyone gives us stuff.

At night, we take the elevator up and down to all the apartments in our building.

Last year, I got a stomachache.

D O N A L D   D I E T Z

Photographer

There is nothing more powerful than Dragon King. Dragon King is so strong he can make the world shake. He breathes fire.

My nickname is Long Fei. It means "flying dragon." For Halloween, I am Long Fei, daughter of Dragon King. So I am also strong and powerful, and tonight I will breathe fire, too.

L I S A   P O W E R S

Photographer

The thing about a ghost is, it can be any-where at any time, like floating over a field of pumpkins or deep in a dark woods, or way up high in a castle.

Ghosts don't usually hide; it's just that people sometimes don't notice them. They are as thin as air and glide around so easily that unless you feel them breathing down your back, you just don't know they're around. *Boo!*

SYLVIA PLACHY

Photographer

One Halloween, there was a little girl named Molly (that's me) who decided to take her grandmother some chocolate-chip cookies and ice-cold milk. She put them in a small picnic basket and put on her red cape. She didn't have to cross any main streets and it wasn't quite dark yet, so her mom said it was okay to go. Along the way, the little girl met up with her best friend, May. Later on, when they met the big, bad wolf, May said, "Go ahead. Give him one of the cookies and he'll go away." Sure enough, May was right. When they got to Molly's grandmother's, she wasn't there. "Probably trick-or-treating," Molly said, and the girls laughed. They sat down on her doorstep and ate up the rest of the cookies and drank down every last drop of the milk.

J O Y C E   R A V I D

Photographer

I can make a dime disappear right out of my hand. My brother told my mom I stole it, but I didn't.

Guess what's under my hat? A tiny, baby-white rabbit. That's what. Of course, these are only tricks. When I grow up, I'll know real magic. Then I'll make my brother disappear.

LYNN GOLDSMITH

Photographer

The thing I'm most scared of is the devil. I think the devil comes out most on Halloween. I'm pretty sure Mr. Fraser is a devil. But there might be more than one. I'm a little scared. But only a little.

When I go out trick-or-treating tonight, I'm with two kinds of people that can scare away devils: a monk and a witch. So that's good.

MAX AGUILERA-HELLWEG

Photographer

I am a witch. Sometimes I am scarier than anyone, and that's when I'm on my broom flying around and screeching. Sometimes I even scare myself. But a lot of the time, me and my cat, Night, just do the normal stuff like laughing in a scary way and stirring up boiling potions in a big pot. Except when the moon is full. Then I am a shadow. Beware.

S H E I L A   M E T Z N E R

Photographer

I sleep in a coffin. And when you all are snuggled in and nighttime is at its darkest, I get up and roam.

This is a warning to Pam Ward and Jessica Briley, who say they're my best friends but who have been telling secrets about me. Watch out!

MARY ELLEN MARK

Photographer

If you are a fairy princess and someone steals you away, no matter how hard a time the prince has, he always finds you. Even if you're way in the back of the darkest forest. And even if you are tired and your hair is so messy your crown falls off, the prince still wants to marry you. The clothes are really nice, too. A fairy princess always lives happily ever after.

E. J. C A M P

Photographer

Teddy gets straight *A*'s and wants to be a doctor when he grows up. I keep my room real neat, feed the dog twice a day, and deliver the evening newspaper to twenty-one houses. Mom says she has the two best boys in town.

But not tonight!

T I M O T H Y   W H I T E

Photographer

It is Halloween night, and in my small village, I will trick-or-treat on horseback. What else? I'm Zorro! My horse, Midnight, knows what to do. We'll start up the dusty road and stop at each of my cousins' houses along the way, and if they don't give me exactly what I want, I might just go **Z** on their fancy shirts.

BARBARA VAN CLEVE

Photographer

My mom says everyone has at least one skeleton in their closet.

I don't know about that, but I know one place I won't be on Halloween . . . and that's in any closet.

PHYLLIS GALEMBO

Photographer

I am your worst nightmare.
  Wrapped in my sheets, I stalk the
inky blackness underground and
rise from the gloom each Halloween.

A R T H U R   T R E S S

Photographer

I thought everyone had to know that one of the worst things you can do on Halloween is to stop a sugarplum fairy and try and have a long conversation with her when she's just on her way out to trick-or-treat. This is the one night when every second counts. This is the night made for sugarplum fairies!

NIGEL DICKSON

Photographer

The moon is full
And I am flying high
As any hairy werewolf might
On a starlit Halloween night.

M I C H A E L   N I C H O L S

Photographer

This year, Buster and Michael are letting me go out with them. Maybe we'll go to the Haunted House first, Buster says. Maybe we won't. The Haunted House is in the gym at the park. Someone told me they blindfold you and make you stick your hands into pots filled with cooked spaghetti and they tell you it's gopher guts. It's all right with me if we don't go to the park, though. I told Buster I wasn't scared or anything, but trick-or-treating is really the fun part of the night. That's what I told Michael, too.

O. E. CATLEDGE

Photographer

I've always wanted to be a rabbit.

Rabbits are soft.

They have puffy tails.

Their ears stand straight up.

They can hide almost anywhere, especially on Halloween.

WILLIAM WEGMAN

Photographer

I felt dumb this year about dressing up. Most of my friends didn't. They had shaving cream and stuff and planned to go out and spray each other. That would be okay. But Liza and I kind of threw something together for costumes, anyway. It didn't seem to matter. I just wanted some candy.

S A L L Y   M A N N

Photographer

Max Aguilera-Hellweg

Max's father was an aerial photographer during World War II. While growing up in southern California, Max practiced with his dad's old Kodak Brownie camera. By the fifth grade he was developing his own film in the bathroom. His first big job after high school was with *Rolling Stone* magazine, for which he photographed Arnold Schwarzenegger. Now he travels all over the world photographing all kinds of subject matter. Because he is Mexican American, many of his photos reflect that cultural background. His books include *Breaking One Hundred*—about people who have lived a century or more.

E. J. Camp

E. J. Camp's photographs have appeared in magazines such as *Harper's Bazaar, US, Esquire, Life,* and *Rolling Stone.* She has also shot photos for movie posters and album covers. In addition she has photographed many celebrities, including Warren Beatty, Nick Nolte, Glenn Close, Robert De Niro, Robin Williams, and Tom Cruise. She currently lives in New York City but would like someday to move back to her hometown in Kentucky.

Oraien Catledge

For more than ten years Oraien Catledge has photographed the people of Cabbagetown, on the edge of downtown Atlanta, Georgia. Cabbagetown is the home of nearly two thousand men, women, and children, and surrounds the once-thriving Fulton Bag and Cotton Mill, whose closing over two decades ago brought about a real crisis in the community. The people in Cabbagetown call Mr. Catledge the Picture Man, and although his vision now is seriously impaired, he has produced more than thirty thousand negatives of this community. The University of Texas Press published *Cabbagetown,* a book of his photos, in 1985, with a foreword by Robert Coles.

Nigel Dickson

In 1977 Nigel Dickson started photographing professionally in Toronto, Canada. Born in 1949 in London, he works primarily in New York, London, and Toronto.

Donald Dietz

Donald Dietz was born in San Francisco and now lives in Hollywood, California. He got his first box camera when he was ten as a prize for subscribing to a newspaper. His photographs have been in thousands of books and magazines. Many of them are in school textbooks. His assignments have given him the opportunity to travel to fascinating places and meet people he would never have met otherwise. Donald especially loves to photograph artists, writers, musicians, and actors. He carries a camera wherever he goes.

Phyllis Galembo

Phyllis Galembo is an associate professor in the art department at the University of Albany, State University of New York, where she teaches photography. She has exhibited, lectured, and traveled widely in the United States and abroad. Her recent book, *Divine Inspiration from Benin to Bahia,* published by the University of New Mexico Press, explores African and Brazilian ritual clothing and shrine objects. Funded by a Polaroid Materials grant, her twenty-by-twenty-four-inch "Skeleton" is part of a larger project using her unique costume collection.

Chuck Gardner

Chuck Gardner was born in the summer of 1952 in Oak Park, Illinois. When he was young he played baseball, rode his bike, and skied. He had no idea that he would ever become a photographer. He now lives in Los Angeles with his wife, Sarah, where they are raising three children. Chuck specializes in advertising photography for the entertainment industry and environmental portraiture. Children have always been one of his favorite subjects. The little boy in his photo for this book is his son, Nicky. They don't know the dog.

Lynn Goldsmith

Lynn Goldsmith is an award-winning portrait photographer and photojournalist. Her acclaimed book, *New Kids,* made publishing history. A regular contributor to the Day in the Life series, she has also produced her own book, *Circus Dreams,* in addition to notable photographic volumes on Bruce Springsteen and the Police (profits from which were donated to Save the Children). Other subjects have included Marky Mark (her most recent book), Richard Gere, Bob Dylan, Tom Wolfe, and Isabella Rosselini.

Mark Hanauer

Mark Hanauer's professional career began as a staff photographer for A & M Records in 1978. Since then, his work has appeared frequently on album covers as well as in *Newsweek, Vanity Fair,* and the *New York Times.* Mark is scared of the dark, so it took a lot for him to go into the darkroom and print his photograph for this book. He trick-or-treats each year with his son, Julian.

Linda McCartney

Linda McCartney grew up in Scarsdale, New York. In 1963 she took a photography class and was so impressed by the photographs of Dorothea Lange and Walker Evans that she dropped out of the class and started photographing full-time. In recent years she has exhibited at the Victoria and Albert Museum in London and at the Royal Photographic Society in Bath. She has published four books of photography and one cookbook for vegetarians. She also plays piano in a band.

Matt Mahurin

Matt Mahurin is an accomplished artist who began his career as an illustrator. He has photographed for many publications, including *Time, Mother Jones,* the *New York Times Magazine,* the *London Sunday Times,* the *Los Angeles Times,* and *Esquire.* His photographic essays have focused on Nicaragua, Haiti, Northern Ireland, the Texas prisons, AIDS, and the homeless. Recently he began translating his haunting visual style to another medium, by directing music videos for Peter Gabriel, U2, Sting, and Tracy Chapman. Born in Santa Cruz, California, in 1959, Mahurin lives in New York City.

Sally Mann

Sally Mann has exhibited her photographs and taught all over the United States. Her work is in the collections of the Metropolitan Museum of Art, the Museum of Modern Art, the Chrysler Museum, and in many other museums and galleries around the country. She has received grants from the National Endowment for the Arts, the National Endowment for the Humanities, the Friends of Photography, and, most recently, the John Simon Guggenheim Foundation. She has three books out; her latest work is titled *Family Pictures.* She lives in Lexington, Virginia, with her husband and their three children.

Mary Ellen Mark

Mary Ellen Mark is a renowned photographer. She has been the recipient of several grants—three from the National Endowment for the Arts—as well as many distinguished photojournalism awards, including the Robert F. Kennedy Journalism Award and the Photographer of the Year Award from the Friends of Photography. Her books include *Passport, Ward 81, Falkland Road, Photographs of Mother Teresa's Missions of Charity in Calcutta, Streetwise, The Photo Essay,* and *Mary Ellen Mark: Twenty-five Years.*

Sheila Metzner

Sheila Metzner took up photography after a career in advertising. Her work has appeared in *Vogue, Vanity Fair,* and many other magazines. Her commercial clients include Fendi, Shiseido Cosmetics, Elizabeth Arden, and Ralph Lauren. Her second photographic book, *Color,* was published by Twin Palms in 1991.

Graham Nash

Graham Nash has been interested in photographs since he was a teenager. Alongside his career as a singer-songwriter, first as a member of the Hollies and later with Crosby, Stills, Nash and Young, the British-born musician also spent much of the last twenty years gathering a large, private photograph collection. Because of the enormous responsibility of caring for these photos, he auctioned them off in 1991. Throughout the years, Graham has always had his own camera with him. In 1991 he debuted his own photographic work in New York City.

Michael Nichols

Michael Nichols was born in Alabama in 1952. He took up photography in college. He was drafted into the army but was able to land a job as staff photographer during his tour of duty. The photos Michael took during that time led to his first professional assignment for *Geo* magazine. Topics for his photographic essays have included: white-water rafting on some of the world's wildest rivers; expeditions in Papua, New Guinea; rappelling off Mount Thor in the Canadian Arctic, and flying into hurricanes with the U.S. Air Force. For the last several years he has worked for *National Geographic.* In 1989 his book *Gorilla* was published. It documents the plight of the mountain gorillas in Africa.

Sylvia Plachy

Sylvia Plachy is a staff photographer for the *Village Voice,* where her regular photographic column,

"Sylvia Plachy's Unguided Tour," has appeared since 1982. Her photographs have been printed in many magazines, including *Vogue, Geo, Camera Arts,* the *New York Times Magazine, Ms.,* and *Newsweek.* In 1977 she received a John Simon Guggenheim Fellowship. Her work is in the collections of the Museum of Modern Art, the Metropolitan Museum, Bibliothèque Nationale, and the San Francisco Museum of Modern Art. Sylvia was born in Hungary and now lives in Queens with her husband and son.

Lisa Powers

Born in Nice, France, and raised in the United States, Lisa Powers began her career in Japan, working for clients such as Issei Miyaki, Eiko Ishioka, Parco, and JVC. She has created memorable images for the *American Film Market,* MTV, and the film *La Femme Nikita.* Her work hangs in the permanent collection of the George Eastman House, as well as in many other private collections. A series of cards with Lisa's images were recently published by Fotofolio.

Joyce Ravid

Joyce Ravid's photographs have appeared in many magazines, including *Time, Newsweek, Condé Nast Traveler, Fortune, GQ,* and *Rolling Stone,* as well as in numerous books. Her own book of photographs, *Here and There,* was published by Knopf in December 1992. Joyce absolutely adores Halloween.

Arthur Tress

Arthur Tress was born in Brooklyn in 1940. He has traveled all over the world photographing people. His first large exhibition and publication was *Appalachia: People and Places.* He has given workshops for schoolchildren, helping them to learn to express themselves more creatively through the imagery they discover in their own dreams. The photograph in *Halloween* is from one of Arthur's books and is entitled "Dream Collection." It was taken in Spanish Harlem on Halloween.

Barbara Van Cleve

Barbara Van Cleve was born in 1933 in Montana, not far from her family ranch. Her parents gave Barbara her first camera when she was eleven. She has always liked to photograph the land: "Its drama and grandeur, the animals, the surprises of weather, and the action of daily ranch life." These things make up the body of Barbara Van Cleve's work, which has illustrated many books and hangs in many galleries.

William Wegman

William Wegman is an artist well known for his paintings and drawings, and even more well known for his photographs of his dogs Man Ray and, more recently, Fay Ray.

Timothy White

Timothy White's portraits have appeared in *Rolling Stone, Parade, US, New York, Condé Nast Traveler,* and in many other magazines. Timothy has also shot the photos that have appeared on a number of movie posters. He studied photography at the Rhode Island School of Design. Later he spent four years as an editorial photographer in South America before returning to advance his career in the United States. He remembers thinking as a child "that skeleton costumes were the coolest—so every year, I dressed up in the same black skeleton suit with sparkles on the bones to reflect the light."

Matt Mahurin